Lucy Can't Sleep

AMY SCHWARTZ

A NEAL PORTER BOOK
ROARING BROOK PRESS
NEW YORK

For Nancy

A Neal Porter Book

Published by Roaring Brook Press

Roaring Brook Press is a division of Holtzbrinck Publishing Holdings Limited Partnership

175 Fifth Avenue, New York, New York 10010

mackids.com

Library of Congress Cataloging-in-Publication Data

Schwartz, Amy.

Lucy can't sleep / Amy Schwartz. — 1st ed.

p. cm.

"A Neal Porter Book."

Summary: Unable to sleep, a little girl tries counting sheep and
other items, searching for her doll and bear, eating a snack, and many
other things in hopes of becoming tired.

ISBN 978-1-59643-543-8

[1. Sleep—Fiction. 2. Bedtime—Fiction.] I. Title. II. Title: Lucy
cannot sleep.

PZ7.S406Luc 2012

[E]—dc22

2011012743

Roaring Brook Press books are available for special promotions and premiums.
For details contact: Director of Special Markets, Holtzbrinck Publishers.

First edition 2012

Book design by Jennifer Browne

Printed in China by Macmillan Production (Asia) Ltd., Kwun Tong, Kowloon, Hong Kong (supplier code 10)

1   3   5   7   9   8   6   4   2

Lucy
can't sleep.

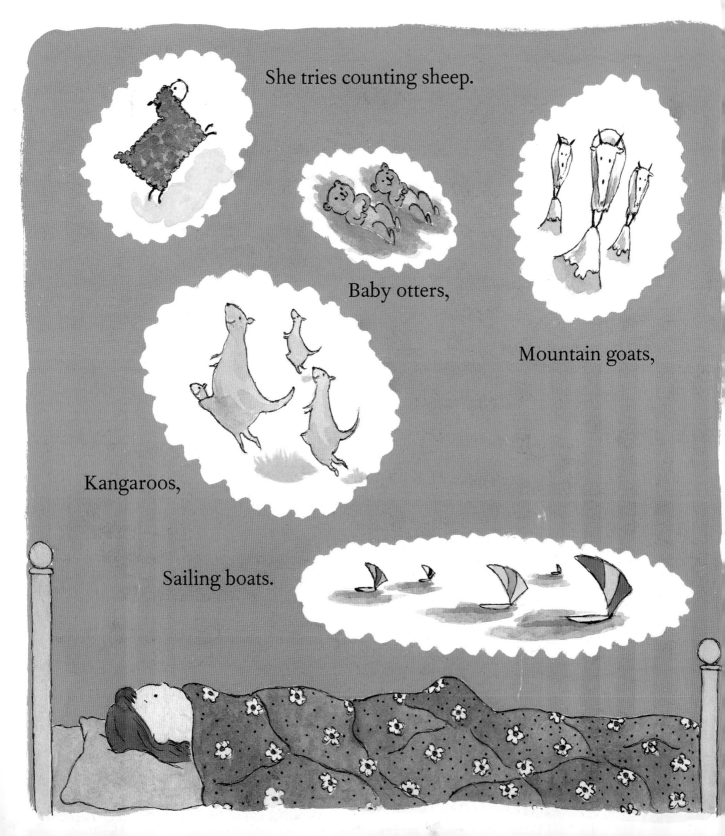

She tries counting sheep.

Baby otters,

Mountain goats,

Kangaroos,

Sailing boats.

Wide-awake Lucy
Climbs out of bed,

Wiggles her fingers,

Wiggles her toes,

Scratches itches,
Itches scratches,

Buttons buttons,

Blows her nose.

Where's Dolly?
Where's Bear?
Lucy looks everywhere.

Way
Up
Here,

And
Way
Down
There.
Where's Dolly?
Where is Bear?

Under this?

Under that?

Inside?

Outside?

In the bath?

Down the hallway?
Down the stairs?

Round the corner?
In the chair!

Lucy,
Dolly, and Bear
Go into the kitchen,
Open the door,
And look in the fridge.

What's inside?

Strawberry shortcake,
Just a bite.
Chocolate pudding,
Quiet night.

A quiet room,
In a quiet house,

A squeaky door,

The back porch.

A comfy swing,
A starry sky,
A radio,
A lullaby.

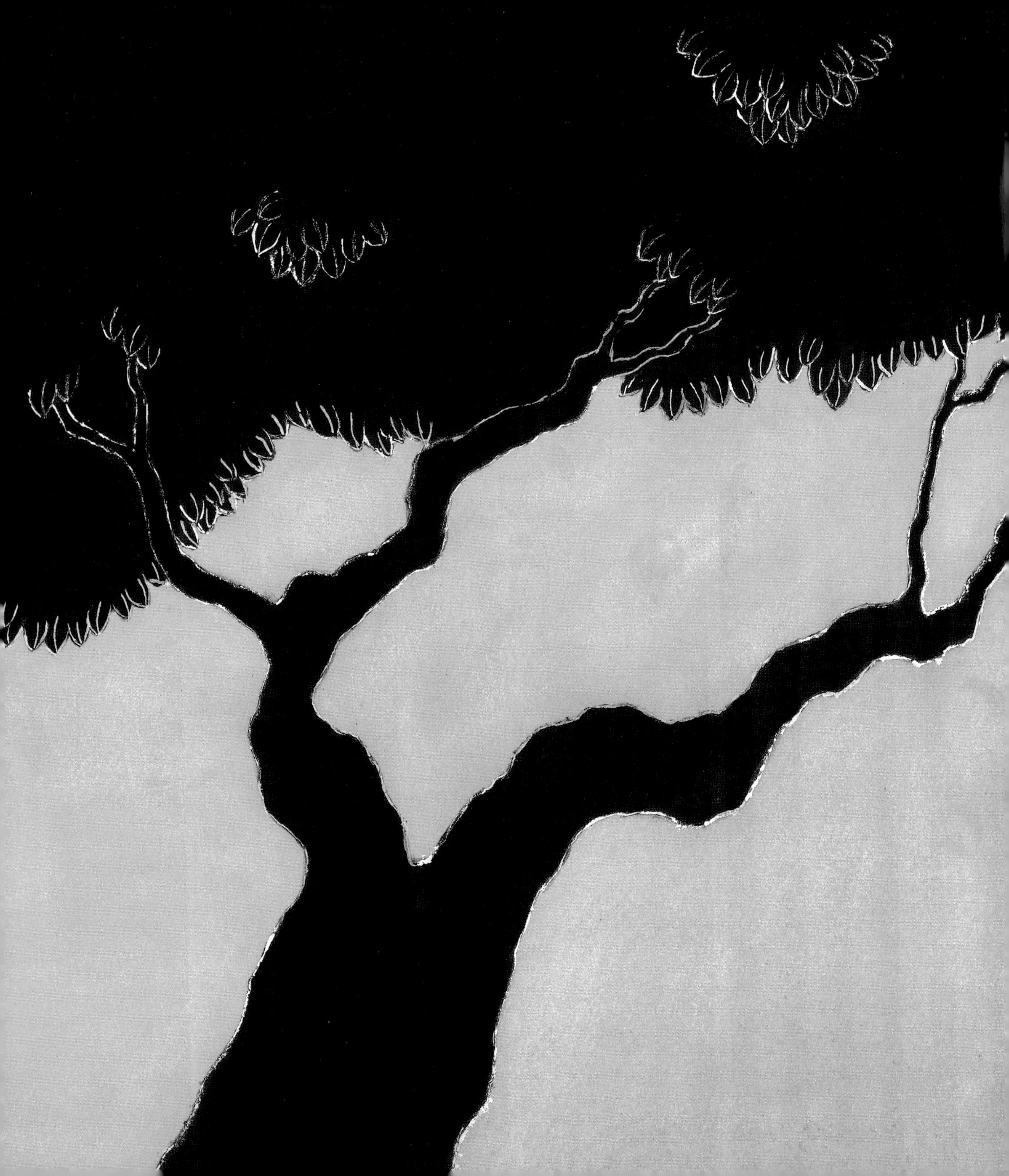

A black tree
With black leaves,
A black squirrel,
A black dog.

A black dog?
A red collar?
It's Lucy's dog!

Come inside.

Lucy and Pup,
Dolly and Bear,
Bumpety-bump,
Climb upstairs.
Upstairs,
Down the hall,
Lucy and Pup,
Dolly and Bear—

Look in mirrors,

Pull out drawers.

Wooly socks,

Slinky scarves,

Fancy shoes,

White gloves.

Lipstick is nice,

So is this hat.

Dance a dance!

Spin around twice.

Sleepy girl,
Sleepy dog,
Sleepy bear,
Sleepy doll,

Slip into bed,
And sleep

'Til dawn.